Impatient Pamela Asks:

Why Are My Feet So Huge?

Trellis Publishing, Inc.
P.O. Box 16141
Duluth, MN 55816

Impatient Pamela Asks: Why Are My Feet So Huge?

Publisher's Cataloging-in-Publication
(*Provided by Quality Books, Inc.*)

Koski, Mary (Mary B.)
    Impatient Pamela asks: Why are my feet so huge?/
by Mary Koski ; illustrated by Dan Brown.
    p. cm.
    SUMMARY: Pamela is unhappy with her larger-than
-average feet, until she realizes what an advantage
they give her in playing youth soccer and other
sports and games.
    LCCN: 98-75352
    ISBN: 0-9663281-2-4

    1. Feet--Juvenile fiction. 2. Soccer for children
--Juvenile fiction. 3. Body image--Juvenile fiction.
I. Brown, Dan (Daniel Seaton) II. Title.

PZ7.K85Imb 1999   [E]
                      QBI98-1573

Soft-cover ISBN:0-9663281-3-2
10 9 8 7 6 5 4 3 2 1

Impatient Pamela Asks: Why Are My Feet So Huge?

Mary Koski

Illustrated by Dan Brown

Dedicated to my six brothers and sisters - the Kleusch clan

M. Koski

Dedicated to children of all ages

D. Brown

It happened on a good day, an ordinary day. Pamela heard the birds singing, she saw the leaves rustling, and she felt the sun shining warm on her face. She and Martin were playing tag.

"You're it!" yelled Martin.

Pamela ran after him and caught him in no time.

"I wish I could run that fast," Martin said. "Maybe if I had such big feet, I could run that fast," he said with envy.

Pamela looked down, and then she saw them, as if for the first time.

"Oh my! Look how HUGE they are!" she screamed.

"Oh, they're not that big," Martin said, putting his foot next to hers.

She ran home. "Momma, look how HUGE my feet are! Why are they so HUGE?"

Pamela's mother laughed and said, "They're a little big. But look on the bright side. They make you special. And you'll grow into them someday."

a didn't want her feet to be different from everyone else's. nted to grow into them RIGHT NOW! She was impatient to grow into the size of her feet.

She sulked for days. She didn't feel like playing with Martin.

And she didn't even pay attention to Meow-Man when he curled up by her side.

"What's wrong, honey?" her father asked. Pamela didn't know what to say. She didn't want to talk about her feet.

"Are you still worried about your feet?" Pamela's mother asked. "Everyone has something that is different from other people. Look at your father. He doesn't like being so tall, but tallness comes in handy."

"And I'm shorter
than I want to be, but
being short helps sometimes."

"Your feet just happen to be a little big, that's all. Look, I made you some peas. That should make you feel better."

But Pamela didn't even want to eat peas.
And she always loved peas.

Finally it was soccer day.
Pamela didn't want to go, but her
mother said it would help to get some
exercise. Pamela always loved soccer
practice. All that running, kicking, and
diving for the ball. Plus she got to be with her
friends. But today she didn't want to be there.

"Why do I have to have such big feet?" she grumbled as she put on her shoes.

She dragged herself onto the practice
field. Her friends waved to her. She
waved back.

"Well, maybe I should try and have
some fun today," she thought.

Pamela and her teammates ran
from one end of the field
to the other,

back and forth.

Pamela got the ball and ran fast. She could move the ball well, because she had a nice big cushion for it. "Great footwork, Pamela," her coach yelled from the sideline.

Pamela looked down. Maybe those feet weren't so bad. After all, they gave her good traction for running, and she could pick up crayons with her toes,

and she could hang upside down on the monkey bars,

and she could use her
feet for snowshoes,

and she could tip-toe in ballet,

and they made good fins for swimming,

and she could stand on tip-toe
and stretch over the counter top to
reach cookies,

and she could handle the ball well.

She took aim at the net and lined the ball up just right on the inside of her foot. She kicked as hard as she could.

The ball went smashing into the net.

GOAL!

"Great aim!" her coach yelled.

"Great feet," Pamela thought.